SKYWALKER STRIKES: VOLUME 2

On the heels of its greatest victory against the evil Galactic Empire, the destruction of the Death Star, the Rebel Alliance is pushing its advantage.

Princess Leia Organa has led a covert team in an attack on Cymoon 1, possibly the largest weapons factory in the entire Empire. Posing as emissaries from an Outer Rim crime syndicate, they gained access and planted charges.

Unfortunately, the "fully automated" factory also contains a number of innocent slave workers. Now, the Rebels race to escape with the freed slaves before the factory is destroyed—a task made far more difficult by the arrival of Sith Lord Darth Vader on the moon....

JASON AARON Writer
JOHN CASSADAY Artist
LAURA MARTIN Colorist
CHRIS ELIOPOULOS Letterer

CASSADAY & MARTIN Cover Artists
CHARLES BEACHAM Assistant Editor
JORDAN D. WHITE Editor

C.B. CEBULSKI & MIKE MARTS Executive Editors
AXEL ALONSO Editor In Chief
JOE QUESADA Chief Creative Officer
DAN BUCKLEY Publisher

For Lucasfilm:
Senior Editor JENNIFER HEDDLE
Lucasfilm Story Group RAYNE ROBERTS, PABLO HIDALGO, LELAND CHEE

ABDO Spotlight

ABDOPUBLISHING.COM

Reinforced library bound edition published in 2017 by Spotlight,
a division of ABDO, PO Box 398166, Minneapolis, Minnesota 55439.
Spotlight produces high-quality reinforced library bound editions for
schools and libraries. Published by agreement with Marvel Characters, Inc.

Printed in the United States of America, North Mankato, Minnesota.
042016
092016

THIS BOOK CONTAINS
RECYCLED MATERIALS

marvelkids.com

PUBLISHER'S CATALOGING IN PUBLICATION DATA

Names: Aaron, Jason, author. | Cassaday, John ; Martin, Laura, illustrators.
Title: Star Wars : Skywalker strikes / by Jason Aaron ; illustrated by Laura Martin and John Cassaday.
Description: Minneapolis, MN : Spotlight, [2017] | Series: Star Wars : Skywalker strikes
Summary: Luke Skywalker and the ragtag rebels opposing the Galactic Empire are fresh off their biggest victory so far-the destruction of the massive Death Star! But the Empire's not toppled yet! Join Luke, Princess Leia, Han Solo, Chewbacca, C-3PO, R2-D2, and the rest of the Rebel Alliance as they fight for freedom against Darth Vader and his evil master, the Emperor!
Identifiers: LCCN 2016932364 | ISBN 9781614795278 (v.1 : lib. bdg.) | ISBN 9781614795285 (v.2 : lib. bdg.) | ISBN 9781614795292 (v.3 : lib. bdg.) | ISBN 9781614795308 (v.4 : lib. bdg.) | ISBN 9781614795315 (v.5 : lib. bdg.) | ISBN 9781614795322 (v.6 : lib. bdg.)
Subjects: LCSH: Skywalker, Luke (Fictitious character)--Juvenile fiction. | Star Wars fiction--Comic books, strips, etc.--Juvenile fiction. | Graphic novels--Juvenile fiction.
Classification: DDC 741.5--dc23
LC record available at http://lccn.loc.gov/2016932364

Spotlight

A Division of ABDO
abdopublishing.com

YOU HOLD THAT WEAPON LIKE AN UNTRAINED CHILD. YOU HAVE NO RIGHT TO IT.
YOU, BOY, ARE NO JEDI.
WHO ARE YOU?
YOU KILLED MY FATHER.
I'VE KILLED VERY MANY FATHERS. YOU'LL HAVE TO BE MORE SPECIFIC.
RRRGGGHH!

UGGH!
THIS IS MOST PATHETIC. YOU ARE NOT WORTH THE *SECONDS* IT WOULD TAKE TO FINISH YOU. WHO SENT YOU HERE TO DIE LIKE THIS?
I WAS *THERE*, ON THE DEATH STAR. I SAW WHAT YOU *DID* TO HIM.
YOU KILLED *MASTER KENOBI!*
AND NOW I'M HERE TO MAKE SURE YOU--
NO!!

SO...OBI-WAN KENOBI GAVE YOU THIS LIGHTSABER. A SHAME HE DID NOT TEACH YOU HOW TO WIELD IT.
HE NEVER DID MAKE FOR MUCH OF A MASTER.
HOW DID YOU...
THE FORCE WILL NEVER BE WITH YOU, BOY. YOUR MASTER HAS FALLEN. WHAT HOPE HAVE YOU?
IF YOU WISH TO LIVE, YOU WILL TELL ME ALL YOU KNOW OF THE REBELLION. INCLUDING THE NATURE OF THIS ATTACK.
AND THEN YOU WILL LEAD ME TO THE REBEL PILOT WHO DESTROYED THE DEATH STAR.
AND WATCH AS I STRIKE HIM DOWN.
SPEAK QUICKLY. OR JOIN YOUR FATHER.
I'D RATHER DIE THAN YIELD TO YOU.
SO BE IT.

WAIT...THIS LIGHTSABER...
I KNOW THIS WEAPON.
THIS ONCE BELONGED TO--

WATCH OUT, KID. THIS THING HANDLES LIKE A DRUNKEN BANTHA.
HAN?!
I'M CLEARING US A PATH OUTTA HERE, LUKE. YOU AND THE REST OF YOUR FRIENDS FOLLOW ME.
OH, CHEWIE WOULD LOVE THIS.
THERE'S VADER! LET'S RAM THIS THING RIGHT DOWN HIS THROAT!
AYE-AYE, PRINCESS.
DEATH TO THE EMPIRE!

UGGH
THIS WAY!
FOLLOW THE WALKER! AND KEEP AWAY FROM--
VADER.
NO.
ALL STORMTROOPERS, REPORT TO MY POSITION AT ONCE.
WE HAVE THE REBELS CORNERED.

NO ONE ELSE DIES BECAUSE OF HIM. I DON'T CARE WHAT HAPPENS TO ME.
HELP ME, BEN. PLEASE...
HELP ME KILL HIM.
KILL THEM ALL.
OR YOU WILL ANSWER TO ME.
OH, BEN.
WHAT HAVE I DONE?

IF YOU'RE GONNA STEP ON SOMEBODY, STEP ON VADER! HE'S THE ONE IN BLACK!
I'M NOT TRYING TO STEP ON ANYBODY. I JUST WANNA GET US OUTTA HERE.
WELL YOU'RE DOING A GREAT JOB OF THAT!
LOOK, DON'T BLAME ME. BLAME THE BUCKETHEAD WHO DESIGNED THIS LUMBERING MONSTROSITY.
WE'RE GOING TO DIE IN THIS MONSTROSITY IF YOU DON'T--
WOULD YOU WATCH WHERE YOU'RE DRIVING, YOU IDIOT?! YOU NEARLY STEPPED ON A TWI'LEK!
THIS IS NOT HELPING! YOU YELLING AT ME IS NOT HELPING! YOU WANNA HELP, SHOOT SOMETHING!
I'D LOVE TO, GENIUS, BUT YOU PICKED A WALKER THAT HASN'T HAD ITS CANNONS HOOKED UP YET!
WE'RE WORKING ON THAT!
RIGHT, GUYS? PLEASE TELL ME WE'RE WORKING ON THAT.
TWEEET BADEEP BRRRRP

ARTOO WILL GET THE CANNONS ACTIVATED. WE JUST HAVE TO GIVE 'EM TIME.
WE DON'T HAVE TIME!
THREEPIO, COME IN! WE NEED THE FALCON! TELL ME YOU'RE EN-ROUTE!
REGRETTABLY, PRINCESS LEIA, THE MILLENNIUM FALCON REMAINS... INDISPOSED.
THE SHIP IS STILL BEING DISMANTLED BY SCAVENGERS. PERHAPS IF YOU OR MASTER LUKE COULD COME TO ASSIST...
THREEPIO, WE'RE TRAPPED IN THIS FACTORY! AND WE'RE ALL GOING TO DIE HERE, UNLESS YOU GET THAT SHIP IN THE AIR!
DO WHATEVER YOU HAVE TO, DO YOU HEAR ME?!
THAT'S AN ORDER!
YES, PRINCESS.
OH.
HOW I WISH ARTOO WERE HERE.
EXCUSE ME.
AH, ATTENTION, SCAVENGERS AND VARIOUS UNKNOWN ALIEN LIFEFORMS. PLEASE REFRAIN FROM FURTHER DISASSEMBLING OF THIS VESSEL.
AND RETURN AT ONCE TO YOUR... DOMICILES. WHEREVER THOSE MIGHT BE. OR ELSE...

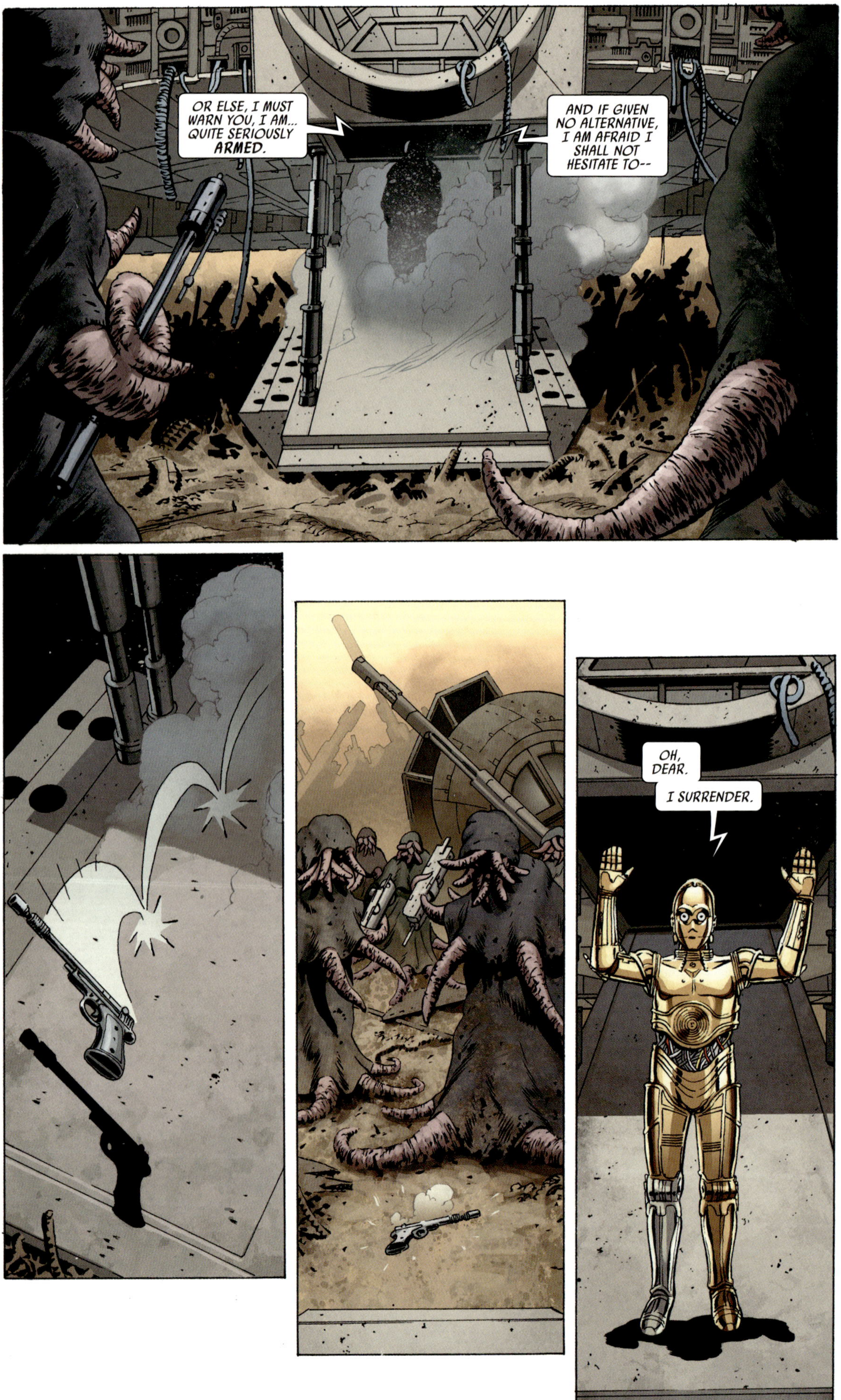

OR ELSE, I MUST WARN YOU, I AM... QUITE SERIOUSLY ARMED.
AND IF GIVEN NO ALTERNATIVE, I AM AFRAID I SHALL NOT HESITATE TO--
OH, DEAR.
I SURRENDER.

SORRY, COULD YOU REPEAT THAT?
I AM FLUENT IN OVER SIX MILLION FORMS OF COMMUNICATION.
DO YOU SPEAK... BOCCE PERHAPS? OR...

STAY DOWN!
WE'LL FIGURE A WAY OUT OF THIS!
WON'T WE?
THIS IS MY FAULT, BEN.
I'M NOT MY FATHER. I'M NOT A JEDI. I'M JUST...
...SOME STUPID FARM BOY FROM TATOOINE. I DON'T BELONG HERE. I DON'T...
YEAH. I'M A FARM BOY, ALL RIGHT.
A FARM BOY WHO CAN BULLSEYE WOMP RATS.

THE REBELS ARE TRAPPED, LORD VADER, BUT WE'LL NEED *ION CANNONS* TO BRING DOWN THAT WALKER.
LEAVE THE WALKER TO ME. JUST MAKE CERTAIN YOU--

THAT BOY...
PERHAPS I WAS TOO HASTY TO DISMISS HIM.
JUST WHAT HAVE YOU BEEN UP TO, OBI-WAN?
NOW I'M TRYING TO STEP ON SOMEBODY.
DO IT. FOR GENERAL KENOBI. FOR ALDERAAN.
NICE KNOWING YA, DARTH.
WAIT...WHY AREN'T WE MOVING? WHAT'S...
YOU GOTTA BE KIDDING ME.

HE'S USING THE FORCE!
HE'S GOING TO TEAR THIS THING APART!
THAT'S NOT POSSIBLE.
THAT'S NOT POSSIBLE! THERE'S NO SUCH THING AS THE FORCE!
TELL THAT TO VADER.
GLADLY.
ARTOO!!
ARTOO! WE NEED THOSE GUNS!
BEEDA BEEDA RREEEEEEEP
WHAT? WHAT'D HE SAY?

HE SAID, "FIRE"!
GGAAAAAGGHH!

ARTOO, YOU BEAUTIFUL DROID, I COULD **KISS** YOU!
WHRRRRP
OH, **HIM** YOU WANNA KISS.
THREEPIO, COME IN! WHAT HAVE YOU DONE WITH MY SHIP, YOU BLITHERING GREASE TRAP?
THREEPIO!?!
SIR, IF YOU'LL NOT BE NEEDING ME...
...I BELIEVE I'LL CLOSE DOWN... FOR A WHILE.
NO WORD FROM CHEWIE OR THREEPIO. **LUKE,** PLEASE TELL ME **YOU'RE** STILL WITH US.
ON MY WAY, HAN. JUST NEED TO PICK SOMETHING UP.

AARRGGHH!
NO SIGN OF VADER. LET'S MOVE OUT.
I DON'T THINK WE'LL BE SEEING ANY MORE OF VADER, KID, NOT AFTER WHAT WE JUST DID TO HIM.
I WISH I COULD BELIEVE THAT...
"...BUT YOU DON'T KNOW THE POWER OF THE FORCE."

LORD VADER, WE HAVE...
HGGGK WHEEZE
MOTHER OF MOONS.
I'M...I'M SORRY, MY LORD. I DIDN'T REALIZE...
GRRK
LORD VADER, THIS IS OVERSEER AGGADEEN.
SIR, I'M AFRAID WE ARE...UNABLE TO HALT THE POWER CORE'S MELTDOWN. REQUEST PERMISSION TO EVACUATE THE FACILITY.
PERMISSION DENIED, OVERSEER. IF THIS FACTORY EXPLODES, YOU HAD BEST EXPLODE WITH IT.
FURTHER FAILURE WILL BE DEALT WITH HARSHLY. THE REBEL INVADERS MUST DIE.
Y-YES, MY LORD.

EXCEPT THE BOY.
LEAVE HIM TO ME.

STAR WARS®

SKYWALKER STRIKES

STAR WARS

SKYWALKER STRIKES

COLLECT THEM ALL!

Set of 6 Hardcover Books ISBN: 978-1-61479-526-1

Hardcover Book ISBN
978-1-61479-527-8

Hardcover Book ISBN
978-1-61479-528-5

Hardcover Book ISBN
978-1-61479-529-2

Hardcover Book ISBN
978-1-61479-530-8

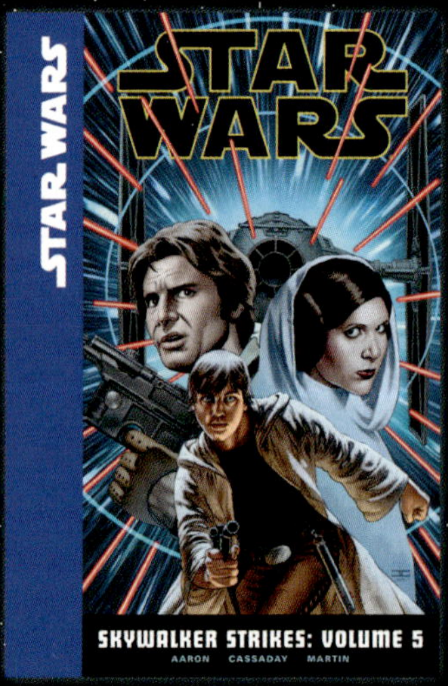

Hardcover Book ISBN
978-1-61479-531-5

Hardcover Book ISBN
978-1-61479-532-2